# I Want To Be

Written by Shawn Rux, PhD

Illustrator: Jonathan M James

This book is dedicated to all the amazing educators out there who make the children they serve feel like they are "the one and only"!

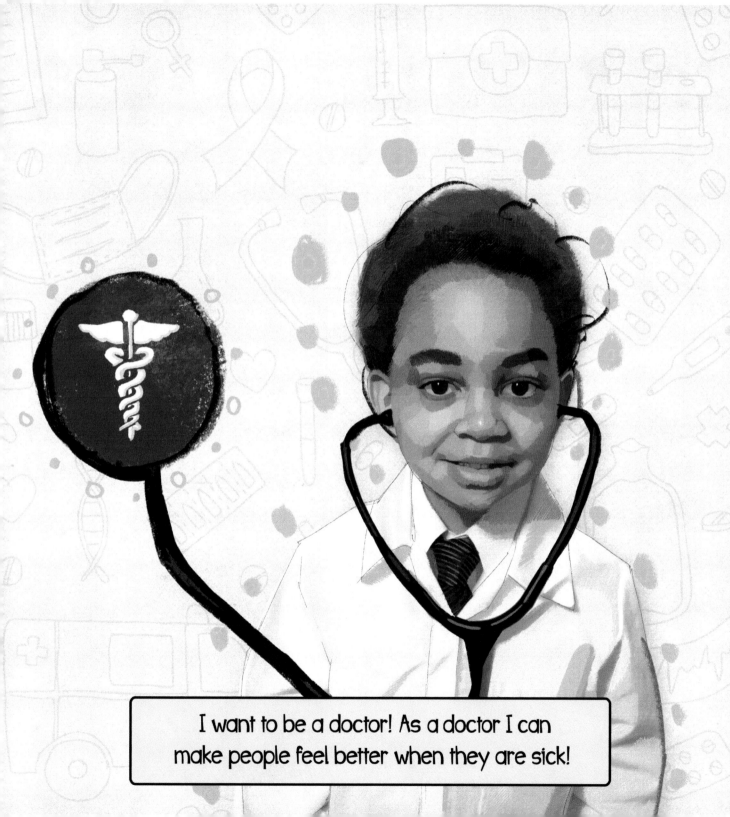

I want to be a doctor! As a doctor I can make people feel better when they are sick!

I want to be a mobile app developer! As a mobile app developer I can provide people with faster service for the things they want and need!

I want to be a judge! As a judge
I can uphold all citizens to obey the law.

I want to be a police officer! As a police officer I can keep my community safe.

I want to be an astronaut. As an astronaut, I can see the entire world and discover new planets!

I want to be a politician! As a politician I can be the president of the United States.

I want to be a video game creator! As a video game creator I can create fun games for people of all ages!

I want to be a fire fighter! As a fire fighter I can put out fires and keep families safe.

I want to be a hairstylist. As a hairstylist I can make everyone look their best.

I want to be a teacher! As a teacher I can help children to be really smart.

What do YOU want to be?
I want to be a _____!
As a _____ I can _____!

Always remember, if you can see it, then you can achieve it!

Name: _____ Date: _____

# I WANT TO BE BECAUSE...

Share more about why you want to be by
completing the sentences below.

I am from


I love


I feel happy when


I think being


I want to make a difference by


I need support


I hope

# I WANT TO BE

My name is _____

I am _____ years old.

I am from _____

I am in Grade: _____

My birthday is: _____

My Self Portrait!

My top 5 favorite activities are:

1. _____

2. _____

3. _____

4. _____

5. _____

I want to be:

I want to be _____

because:

Name: _____ Date: _____

# GOAL
# SETTING

Think about **what you want to be** and write down three goals for the new school year.

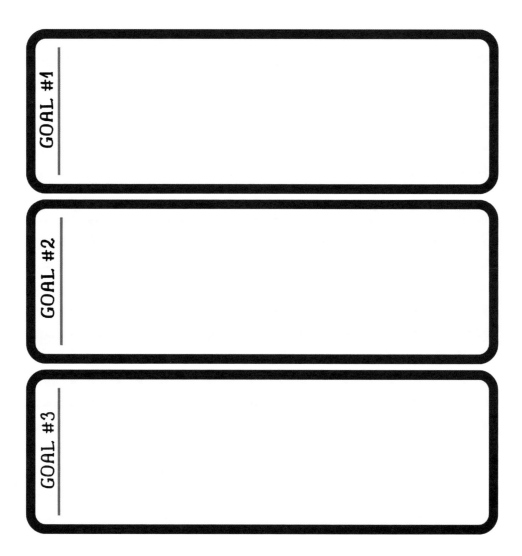

GOAL #1

GOAL #2

GOAL #3

You are a kid now, but one day you
will be a grown up with a career!
It's never too early to begin thinking about
what you want to be when you grow up!